Novel Ideas

Also By K. B. Dixon:
The Photo Album
The Ingram Interview
A Painter's Life
Andrew (A to Z)
The Sum of His Syndromes
My Desk and I

Novel Ideas

a novel

K. B. DIXON

Baffling Bay Books

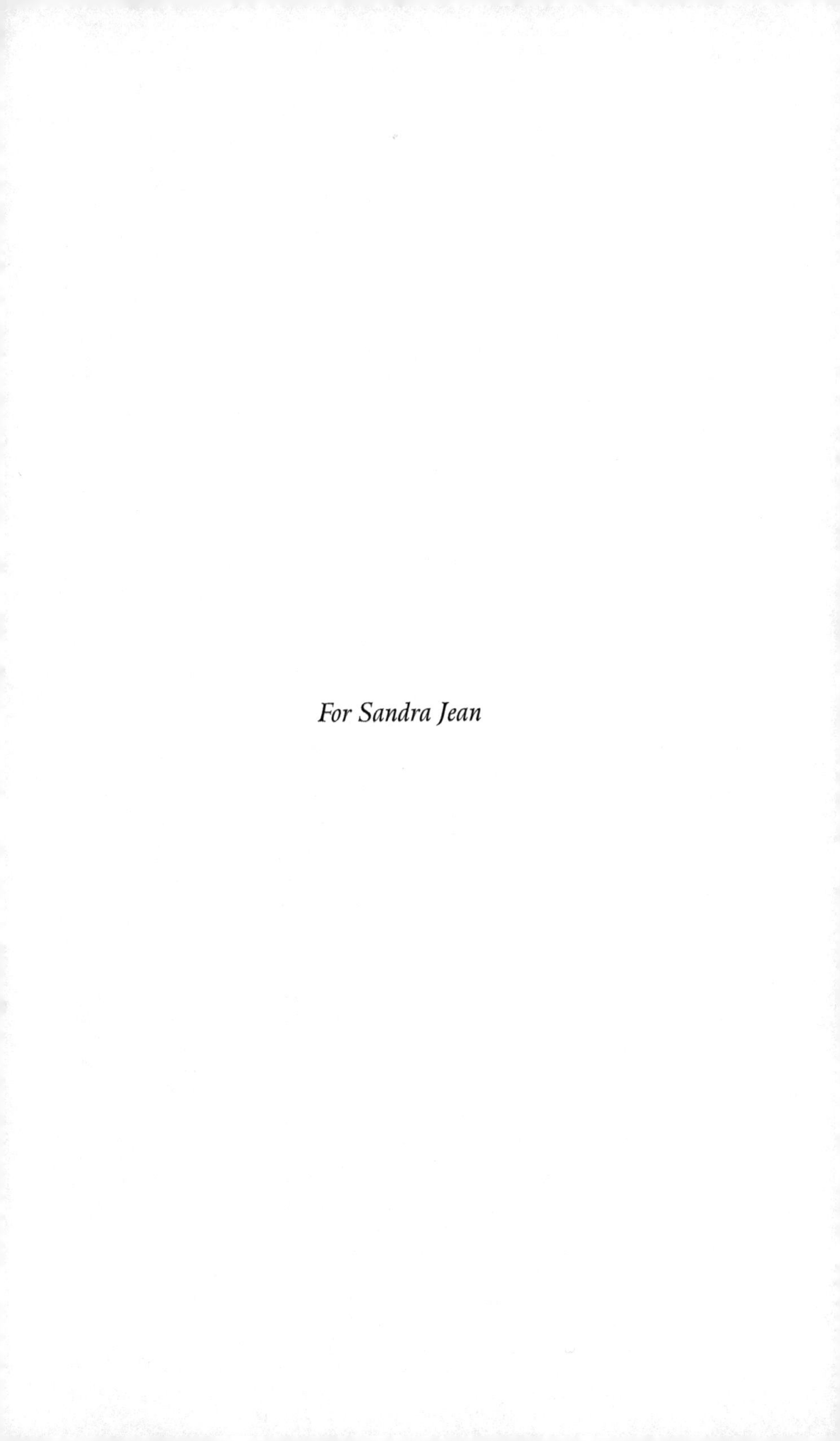

For Sandra Jean

Introduction

Two years ago at the urging of his tax attorney, Stephen Styles, an obscure Seattle writer of unconventional fiction, donated his papers to the University of Washington for a piddling but, nonetheless, welcome tax deduction. These papers, such as they were, might have suffered the fate of similarly insignificant caches and languished unexamined in perpetuity were it not for the collective industry of an especially energetic gaggle of graduate students (Advanced Library Science 501) whose quaint scholarly aspirations encouraged the zealous practice of their dark arts on whatever meager materials might be at hand.

This book, the product of that industry, is a judiciously abridged version of this ambitious group's thesis project. A collection of excerpts from letters and emails written by Mr. Styles to his close friend, the novelist Alan Dodd, it offers us a look at the author and his tentative foray into nonfiction from an unusual and, I think, informative angle.[1]

Dr. Arthur Crimmons
Department of Library Science
University of Washington

---

[1] I would be remiss if I did not mention here that Mr. Styles was asked in advance of publication to supply additional contextualizing commentary, but he declined. While I, of course, respect his decision on the matter, I cannot feign an unconflicted endorsement of it.

1

Alan, that was a terrific review of *Conversations*. You must be pleased. I liked the part about you being "quizzical, modern, and urban." How does it feel to see your name in the same sentence as Calvino's?

I am in the dumps again this morning. This book I'm working on, the one I mentioned to you—the phony, upside-down and backwards memoir—is making me very unhappy. It's not cooperating. Also, there is Aaron (the publisher du jour) who has been hinting for some time now as diplomatically as he can that the new reality of the book business has made taking on marginal projects like the ones I offer a harder and harder thing to do.

⁕

Natalie and I had one of our talks last night. She insists on them occasionally and—I must reluctantly admit—for good reason. I have certain obsessive tendencies, and she feels compelled from time to time to reorient me. She is worried. She thinks I have been getting conspicuously and intransigently stranger, that certain psychic requirements are becoming borderline pathological (for example the anti-social inclinations, the need for serenity and seclusion). She thinks I have been slipping little by little, book by book, and that something in this latest effort of mine has taken me over some edge. (It feels a little that way to me as well.) She had an idea. Maybe I should take a little time off—not just from my formal fiddling with the epistemological puzzles of narration, but from fiction in general—time off from imaginary people and imaginary experiences. Maybe I should try something "conventional," reportorial, nonfictional—get in touch, even if just obliquely, with the real world again. She has always had a lot of faith in the real world.

It looks like Russell Walker has finally decided to give us a memoir. I suspect he will be well served by the general public's insatiable appetite for scurrilous detail. Right now, as I understand it, his focus is on his relationship with his mother. That could be a book by itself. I assume he will succumb to temptation and give us a page (or three) on the genetic basis of various personality disorders.

Jason Hedges's son Peter has signed up for an evening class in screenwriting at the Pacific Northwest Film Center. The class is being taught by Evan Hunter, an iffy character with an extravagantly imagined resume. The classroom itself is a standard-looking one—ugly, functional, all hard surfaces—the sort of place that is easy to hose out.

Natalie's sister Allison (the one I told you about who lives in Portland) is apparently in one of her distant and distracted moods. She is perplexed by the world and everyone in it—including her kids, which, of course, is understandable. This mood—which is becoming a perpetual one for her—

was triggered in part, I think, by the impending arrival of her parents. They will be visiting for a week. She and her husband John are meeting them at the airport tomorrow. (I don't think there is a place on earth that I like less than an airport.)

Robert, my morbid father-in-law (who I think is growing more morbid by the week), has never seemed all that comfortable with Allison. He thinks she has a devious nature. Needless to say he and John don't get along. Natalie has advised Allison to prepare herself for the usual sort of thing, but she has not—which means, I guess, we should expect her to be upset and to have had her feelings hurt by the time they get to baggage claim.

⋅◉⋅

Unfortunately, it looks like the Walker book is going to be just what I feared—mind-numbingly thorough. As a reader, I can't think of anything that has done more damage to the art of biography than the pedantic pursuit of definitiveness. Right now Russell is ankle-deep in elementary-school lore. It's not my eyes, but my brain that glazes over. According to RW (if you read between the as-yet unpolished lines), it was his early failure as an athlete that doomed him to a life of compensatory excess.

Peter's rough-draft screenplay is about a chemist who loses his mind. He is doing drug research (on a supposedly side-effectiveless antidepressant) with an imaginary lab partner named Arthur—an apparition who likes classical music and smells of cinnamon.

Allison's father always tries to look happy to see his son-in-law, but he never quite succeeds. John wonders why he bothers. He stopped playing that game with Robert a long time ago. If there are a number of things about Allison to which her father objects, there are more than a number of things about John. His hair style, for example. Robert finds it leftish and, consequently, provocative.

The more I think about that idea of Natalie's, the more I like it. I have over the years (apparently like everyone else) found myself being drawn in my reading life more and more toward nonfictional work. I've been attracted in particular to the literary variants of the "true crime" genre.

I am probably not the best judge of this sort of thing (as I am rarely able to engage with the mom-and-pop parts of these bios), but I think Walker is overworking the backstory—Patricia Walker's especially. I am not really that interested in the pre-Russell lives of his mother and father—in what was done to them. I am interested in what they did to him. I know Patricia is important (I can't think of any fiction more cravenly autobiographical than Walker's), but do I really need to know about a distant genealogical relationship to Daniel Boone or a date with Adam West (the actor who played Batman on television)?

Allison's parents flew back to KC yesterday. The night before, she and John took them out to dinner. Robert ordered steak (he finds scallops, stuffed sole, and crab effeminate). The dinner conversation was a familiar one—an inquiry into John and Allison's current financial situation; questions about the kids (Justin and Hailey); and a dithering, dyspeptic disquisition on Second Amendment rights as set forth in the U.S. Constitution.

Have you heard any more from your frightening fan—what was her name? Leah Keen? I know your initial response to her flattering note was simply a common courtesy, but, as I said at the time, one rarely regrets a defensive restraint. Good manners are unusual. They have of late become even more so. Fewer and fewer people know how to interpret them.

Natalie came home tonight with two cantaloupes. They are the size of bowling balls. They look like experiments. I'm afraid to eat one.

Peter has introduced me to some of his classmates and their screenplays:

Rebecca Sykes, a chewing-gum snapper, is working on a movie told mainly in flashbacks. A young girl sits in prison talking to a priest about killing her parents. She has had help from a boyfriend—a tattooed, knuckle-dragging, drug addict who dreams (predictably enough) of being a rock star. The story moves back and forth between then and now—

between the murder of the parents and this young lady's present-day life in prison, a life populated and defined by dictatorial guards and domineering inmates. There is a friend in the cell next door, Edith Springs. A one-time cake decorator, she has also been incarcerated for murder.

Amanda Green, dental hygienist, is working on a movie about a courageous single mother who lives in a small town. She loses her job when the box-manufacturing plant where she works shuts down. Looking for a way to support herself and her daughter Amy (curly brown hair, strawberry allergy), she comes up with the idea of building a kennel in her backyard and breeding show dogs—Dalmatians. She fights first with the city for a permit, then with the bank for a loan. Eventually, as she struggles to get the business going (construction cost overruns, vet bills), there are threats of foreclosure. One of her dogs, Fitz (named after Fitzwilliam Darcy, the romantic lead in Jane Austen's *Pride and Prejudice*), is entered in a large and prestigious county show. He is pitted against the pampered pup of a privileged, manicured, Mercedes-owning Maureen Hillwood. He wins. Everyone lives happily ever after.

Martin Whately, ping-pong prodigy, is doing a science-fiction piece. Served warm on a voice-over bed of misunderstood Nietzsche, it includes an army of slime-oozing aliens and a clowder of augmented starlets.

I am never going to get used to this new washing machine. One of the cycles is "Berserk." It lulls you in the beginning with a sort of gentle, sloshing, metronomic rock-a-bye—then suddenly somewhere around minute eighteen, it goes crazy—it starts shaking and jumping up and down hysterically. I wouldn't be surprised to hear of it registering on nearby seismographs. It's a mind mangler.

Walker's mother is one thing; his aunt is another. It is a mystery to me—men and women who marry in desperation when it is so easy to simply adopt a dog.

Here, as a reader, are the basic familial relationships listed in order of interest (for me anyway):

Mother/Daughter

Father/Daughter

Mother/Son

Father/Son

Dinner at Oboe's with the Motts—which brings me to a sensitive subject, a recurring issue in this charmed circle: dessert. No one but me ever wants to order one, so I am given carte blanche. Unfortunately, whatever I order will not, in the end, be mine. When it arrives everyone will remark on how good it looks and eventually jump in for a bite or two. I come up three-quarters of a dessert short. This has happened often enough for me to develop a defensive strategy: I have changed what I order. Now it is not necessarily what I want or what sounds best to me, but what seems likely to be largest.

I am taking my preliminary plans for an exploratory trip into nonfiction over to my old mentor, John Hyde. Two reasons: one, I could use a few words of encouragement (Dr. H has of late become something of a campus provocateur suggesting that the novel as we know it is now basically passé), and two, the good doctor's daughter, Miranda, is married to a police detective. An introduction to someone with expertise and information that they might be willing to share would be a good place to start.

2

I don't think you have ever met Dr. Hyde. Hydrocephalic, balding—he looks like a bearded lightbulb. With tenure he now has a new office. It reminds me of his old one (a book-lined storage closet) except it has a window—a small one that looks out on a patch of green common where lithe young women chase Frisbees while their tattooed, less-lithe boyfriends petition passerbys to save the whales, fight corporate greed, and recall the reactionary governor of South Carolina.

We didn't talk that much about my project. He was scheduled to meet with a visiting literatus at one of the department's sycophantic shindigs and was distracted. (He is a lot better than me at that sort of thing, but he is still not what you would call an accomplished schmoozer.) He does not in his late middle-years have the same sort of star-struck admiration of eminence that he had in his youth, and he suspects that when introduced to a man who reflexively anticipates astonishment and applause, he will disappoint as he will not to be able to simulate accurately the sort of enthusiasm expected. But he did offer an introduction to Kevin, his son-in-law, the police detective.

For some reason my niece Hailey has gotten interested in her vocabulary. She has been working to improve it. She thinks Allison, John, and Justin should be working on theirs as well. She gives them a new word every day. They have to use it in a sentence. Today the word was "doleful." John gave her a look rather than a sentence. This exercise—new words and using them in sentences—is supposed to improve one's ability to express oneself. John told her that he wasn't sure doing a better job of that would be helpful.

Walker is worried about his daughter. She is precocious and apparently wants to be a writer, and he is concerned already about how he will be portrayed in her first novel.

Peter Hedges was for a very short time attracted to one of the young ladies in his screenwriting class—a singer, Niki Holman, who knows how to wear a black sweater and whose movie, as it turns out, was heavily autobiographical. (It is the story of her musician boyfriend's suicide or, more accurately, the story of her theatrical reaction to her musician boyfriend's suicide.)

Niki read a scene from her script—a scene where her lead visits the dead boyfriend's mother to collect a vial of his cremated ashes, which she intends to scatter on a beach near Haystack Rock. X thought it was a wonderful scene. Y thought it was a wonderful scene. Z thought it was a wonderful scene. Paul Fennell, the class's lone cinesthete, thought its reliance on textural signifiers was dated. Peter offered a cautious criticism—said it seemed a bit exploitive, that the solipsistic focus on the female character's struggle with grief puts her in danger of losing some obviously much sought-after sympathy. It was not a criticism that Niki took well.

My niece's latest vocabulary word: "disgruntled." I thought immediately of her grandfather. He golfs weekly with a squad of aging malcontents. They like nothing better on Wednesday mornings than to wander the links complaining about the state of pretty much everything. They punctuate their postmortems with angry tee shots and hostile drives. Most of the conversations seem to revolve around Republican politics and personal health issues—tax policy and by-pass operations (whose was most significant—who had a double, who had a triple, who had a quadruple). From time to time there are detours into domestic issues, expressions of various sorts of disappointment—complaints about sons; daughters; wives; and, of course, we familial extensions. I expect they must compare unsatisfactory grandchildren as well.

❧❦❧

I met with Kevin Cain today (Hyde's detective son-in-law). Not a hard-boiled sort at all—no broad shoulders, cleft-chin, hairy back, Meerschaum pipe, or bumbling sidekick. Sort of soft-boiled—with a buzz-cut. He looks like the guy who does your taxes. I explained to him as best I could what I was looking for in the way of a subject for this book of mine—something unsolved, something ungory. He said to give him a couple of days. He would see what he could come up with.

I heard Natalie and Allison talking on the phone again last night about their long lost dreams of being veterinarians. (Natalie small animals, Allison large.) It's a discussion that seems to be had regularly. No one who loves animals the way they do could ever be wholly indifferent to human beings the way...say, Dr. Roty is.

Most of their time though was spent talking about Elizabeth Lee. Her husband died recently. (They always seem to know someone whose husband died recently.) Apparently Mrs. Lee has lost a part of her mind. She has been wearing the dear departed's favorite suit to bed at night.

Unlike Walker, I have had few brushes with the rich and famous—the sort of thing that gets him so excited. I have never lived near an abstract expressionist, eaten breakfast with a disgraced congressman, or shared a stage with the heir to a European chocolate fortune.

That was an interesting note you received from your fan Ms. Keen about meeting for a cup of coffee. I am sure you don't need me to suggest that you decline; you might, however, need me to suggest that you decline a little more fulsomely than you are by nature prompted. I know you would not be rude, but I suspect you might be succinct, and I would suggest that concision in a case like this is very likely to be misconstrued—to be experienced as something other than a courtly demonstration of linguistic facility.

Peter is fascinated with Evan Hunter, the man teaching his screenwriting class. Apparently he sweats a lot, owns a pistol, and cannot swim. He is seeing a younger woman—Anna Yaw whose complex hairdo is the product of much desperate experimentation. She is interested it seems in only three things: her appearance, other people's opinions of her appearance, and Elvis Presley—who she is convinced would have lived and thrived and made hundreds of young women just like her deeply happy if he had eaten right and exercised. Her obsession with this fantasy figure is fervent. Just the thought of him changes her brain chemistry for the day. Evan claims to be amused by this infatuation, its quaintness, its ardor, but he is, in fact, jealous. He never misses an opportunity to say something malicious about the man—a habit that led to ugly arguments and eventually the dissolution of the relationship.

From time to time Natalie will pick up a stray idea and worry it smooth—like a river rock. The current concern is with our hot-water heater. She has decided it is old and might explode. We are having it looked at.

Walker is lucky. The man can write quite beautifully. His style carries the reader through his more trying pages—the over-researched and analyzed teen years for instance.

I have always had an interest in movies. I was at one time, in fact, contracted to adapt a short story of mine—*Lost Earrings*. A young would-be auteur by the name of Colin Forrestal bought the rights to the story for not very much and asked me to write the script (also for not very much). I agreed.

The story—a cryptic and oblique look at emotional inattention—did not really lend itself to dramatization, but I did what I could. Mr. Forrestal reportedly liked the pages I supplied and was negotiating with a reasonably well-respected character actor for the lead when something happened and the project came to a halt. (Shortly thereafter, as I understand it, Mr. Forrestal folded up his movie-making tent and headed off to law school.)

⁕

It will be interesting to see what Walker does with his stint at *Metro Magazine* as a restaurant reviewer. (His *nom de plume* was Mr. Dishing It Out.) I've actually read a few of those reviews. They are trivial but fun.

⁕

I've never used the word "sapling" in a story. Have you?

⁕

Kevin Cain dropped by the house last night with a case file on the murder of a gallery owner named David Charter. It has been open for a year and a half. A handsome, fastidious, greyhound-thin, fifty-two-year-old, Charter was found dead in his downtown apartment. He had been poisoned.

I spent the morning doing what I do best—avoiding work on the work-in-progress. There are these letters to you, and now it seems I've been making some notes for a new novel—a novel about a bookkeeper.

3

I have been familiarizing myself with both the Charter case and this new genre. I've combed the file thoroughly and forced myself through a half-dozen gruelingly pedantic "How To" books. I have been encouraged by several masters of the interview to buy a voice recorder. It is apparently a writing aid, a legal necessity, a symbol of seriousness. (I am also supposed to think a little about my style of dress. Jeans and sweatshirts are fine for fiction, but nonfiction—especially nonfiction when interviews are involved—requires something a little more formal. Pants with creases in them, shirts with collars.)

Allison is worried about one of Hailey's new friends. (I think her name is Morgan, but it could be Chloe.) She says this girl is too sophisticated for her daughter, that the information and opinions she is passing on are growing Hailey up a little too quickly. She—Allison—is not really sure how to best handle this. She knows her disapproval will only make this girl more interesting. Doing nothing evidently is not an option. John, she says, is no help at all.

I tried in vain to talk Natalie out of watching this evening's news. Expect a lot of muttering, head-shaking, and numerous exasperated exhalations.

Walker has come to his first meeting with Julia—at a party, of course. This means we will be getting a few pages about Julia's mother and father. I have no doubt that Walker will want to portray her as an unhappy and tormented character.

I made a trip to one of those office-supply stores today—cavernous, linoleumed, cruelly overlit. What I wanted was someone with expertise, someone who could narrow down the options for me, someone who could point me toward the voice recorder best suited to my needs. But, of course, expertise is not really something you are going to get in a store like this—not with what they pay. What you get is the usual—a young man in a white, translucent, short-sleeved shirt (the sort of thing that comes in packages of three and does not look like it could possibly survive more than a half-dozen wash cycles) who appears under this leaching fluorescent light to be suffering from some sort of vitamin deficiency. He has been told by management to be helpful and he tries, but he doesn't really know much of anything about anything—not even the geographic location of the merchandise in question. The best he can do is simulate helpfulness, which means in the end when he eventually does locate the recorders (hidden over between the label-makers and paper-shredders), he can only read bullet points off the packaging in answer to my questions.

Natalie is across the street visiting the irrepressible Isabel Bennett. She is somebody's grandmother—we are not sure whose. (It has been explained, but none too clearly.) Natalie goes weekly for the conversation—Isabel is very smart and very funny—but she also goes for Willy (short for Wilhelm), Isabel's German Shepherd. She takes Bobby, our beagle, with her. We have been told he needs a few friends of the same species, that it is good for his mental health.

My notional bookkeeper's name is Ethan Davis. He works at Perkins & Perkins, a small but intrepid plastics manufacturer. Tomorrow is his birthday. He will be 35. It doesn't seem possible. His life is slipping away. He doesn't know what is going on. He thinks maybe if he ran some numbers he might get a better idea.

According to the Center for Something Something, the average life expectancy right now for someone like Ethan—if they slept well, worked average hours, didn't smoke, drank little coffee, exercised regularly, took calcium, stayed out of the sun, wore a seatbelt, and avoided red meat—would be 75. (Actually it would be 75.7, but Ethan rounds down because he is a pessimist.) If he had some hard data, if he knew how he had been spending his time, maybe he could save some of it—in effect, extend his life—make up for some of what he has wasted. It wouldn't be enough for a whole second chance, but maybe it would be enough for part of one. If he considers a "day" to be 24 hours (that is a day and a night), then at 35 Ethan has lived 12,775 of them. He can expect to live only 14,600 more.

More notes on my calculating bookkeeper:

WIFE

Ethan is not married and, as he understands it, this counts against him. If he gets married sometime in the near future, he suspects he could pick up some of the purported actuarial benefit. He makes a note to himself: "Send flowers to Ashley." (She should have Natalie's smile.)

SLEEP

Right now Ethan gets about 7 hours of sleep a night—that is about 106 days and nights of sleep a year. If he cuts his sleeping down to 6 hours a night he would save about 365 hours a year or about 15 days. That means in the time he supposedly has left, Ethan could extend his conscious life by about 20 months or almost 2 years. Of course he would have to give up some of these savings to the health problems that are related to a lack of sleep, but he doubts he would have to give up all of them. He can't imagine more than two-thirds. A gain of only 5 days a year of discretionary sentience would, in the end—that is, from now until the bitter end—mean an extra 6 ½ months to him.

One of Walker's "revelations" is about the early influence of Salinger. Is this really a revelation? What writer of Walker's generation (or the generation after, for that matter) did not pass through their Salinger phase. (It really kills me when ole Walker says something like that.)

WORK

Ethan works a standard shift at Perkins & Perkins—which is 40 hours a week—time that is not consequently available for doing anything important with his life. He gets 2 weeks of vacation and 1 week worth of holidays. This means that in a year Ethan works about 2000 hours or 83 days and nights. Assuming he will retire at age 66, this job will cost him another 60,000+ hours or 2,573 days. Of course, there are all sorts of unspecified benefits—food, shelter, health insurance. He would guess he gets back—in unspecified ways—about half of this loss, but, of course, there is room here for debate.

The average daily commute (if there are no accidents on Highway 26) is about 70 stressful minutes. That works out to 12 days a year—a figure that should probably be doubled given the purpose of his calculations here. This means a loss from now until retirement of an additional 744 days and nights.

Personal Hygiene

Ethan spends about 4 minutes a day brushing his teeth—2 in the morning and 2 at night. This means that in the course of a year he spends a full day at just this task. From now until the end (assuming Ethan keeps his teeth), he loses 40 days. He should add a few additional days to that loss—say 7—as there are invariably times when he brushes his teeth more often, more than just in the morning and at night. He should also add time spent at the dentist. Ethan has so far kept that to a minimum. Assuming his luck will hold (and there is no reason to believe it will), he would say he averages about 3 hours a year there. (This includes the time spent thumbing old magazines in the waiting room.) That, from the beginning to the end, is another 5 days. Total number of days lost to dental-related issues: 52.

Ethan showers and washes his hair every day. It takes about 15 minutes—10 showering, 5 hair-washing—which means he spends about 4 days a year doing this or 160 days from now until the end. If he starts washing his hair every other day instead of every day, Ethan would over the next 40 years save about 600 hours or 25 days and nights. Similarly, shaving every other day would save him a like number: 25 days.

❦

I think Natalie may have a mutant gene—one that produces a mosquito-attracting pheromone. She buys calamine lotion by the liter and uses the word "Florida" as an expletive.

❦

Walker has, without question, a flair for descriptive prose. Unfortunately, I don't know if, in this image-addled day and age, that is quite the advantage it used to be.

❦

I think John is concerned about Justin—that he might not be an insightful person. He might not be. I can't remember him ever saying anything imaginative or discerning. He does seem to have a tenacious streak though—that can make up for a lot. As for Hailey—she is another story. She is very smart and very pretty. Will she use her powers for good or for evil? Only time will tell.

I had an unusual experience today. I was walking back to the car after a late lunch with Bill Simmons (tacos and tequila) when a young lady photographer packing several pounds of expensive-looking camera stopped and asked to take my picture. My first reaction, of course, was to say "no," but there was something about the way she inflected the question that made me hesitate. I asked her why she wanted to take my picture and she said she didn't exactly know— that at first it was my hat (I was wearing that Irish slouch thing), but it was more than that, something else, an individual response. There was something about me that seemed interesting and was graphically articulated (whatever that means). She had a certain earnest sincerity about her that the cynic in me could not entirely dismiss. I consented. She took her picture (which will end up god knows where), thanked me, and headed off down the street. I hope at some point it will be converted from cretinish color into honest black and white.

I agree this is not a good sign—Ms. Keen asking you questions about your personal life, about your relationship with your mother and father. What next? Your home phone? Your Social Security number?

◦◉◦

Dodging the blank page again this morning—insisting that I can do otherwise but not doing otherwise, being who I am though I wouldn't mind at all (for the moment anyway) being someone else.

◦◉◦

Another conference with Dr. Hyde. He showed me his new watch, a gift from his daughter who disapproved of but (out of love) acquiesced to his almost demonic obsession with time. It is a huge thing, this watch—the size of a saucer. Liberally decorated with knobs and dials, it looks both expensive and accurate. It tells Hyde the time not only here but in Tokyo, London, Paris, and Sydney. It looks like something it would take the congenitally predisposed weeks to master. Hyde uses it to orient himself not only temporally— as the earth spins on its axis and orbits an indifferent sun— but actuarially. A fervent and practicing hypochondriac, he stares at its exquisitely polished face and follows the graceful sweep of its second hand as he checks his own pulse. This is something I've seen him do before, but never with quite the same concentration.

I thumbed through an anthology last night. I think it was Shakespeare who said there was never yet a philosopher who could endure a toothache patiently. From the evidence here it looks like the same thing could be said about writers and automobile accidents. Fender-benders to fatalities—nothing gets less than 1500 words.

The trick in this new book will be to lower expectations at the beginning so that what follows will be experienced as something better than it is.

4

According to Charter's file it was Karen Young, one of the assistants at his gallery, who discovered his body. Charter had missed a morning meeting with one of his artists, a disgruntled neo-expressionist by the name of Robert Hill-wood. When Charter did not answer his phone, Ms. Young walked over to his apartment. (It was just a few blocks from the gallery.) She knocked. There was no answer. She looked through the glass at the side of the front door and saw Charter, naked, biscuit-dough white, lying dead in the living-room. I have made arrangements to interview her.

Did you ever have a rabbit when you were a kid? I did. As I remember, a neighbor's dog got into the backyard and ate it. Justin has been petitioning for one. He is very enthusiastic. Nobody knows where he got the idea. Allison says "yes." (She always says "yes.") She thinks it will teach her son responsibility. John says he wants to think about it (his diplomatically diluted version of "no"). I remember being amazed by the softness and the aliveness of the thing—amused by its method of locomotion and its passion for lettuce. John fears the enchantment will be short-lived and that the relationship will end badly for everyone.

Still imagining my bookkeeper and his doomsday spreadsheet.

EXERCISE

Ethan exercises 45 minutes a day, 3 times a week, which means he spends 5 days a year at it. From now to the end—that would be 200 days. He expects this number to be a little smaller though because he expects the time he spends exercising will decrease as he gets older, so let's say he will have spent 150 days at it by age 75. Certain fanatics have tried to convince us that for every hour spent exercising, one gains an extra half-hour of life, but Ethan doesn't really believe this. For argument's sake let's get all optimistic and say he will gain an extra quarter-hour of life for every hour spent exercising—that would mean an addition of about 37 days.

PREPARING AND CONSUMING MEALS

Ethan is not much of a breakfast eater. Breakfast for him usually means peeling a banana or popping the top off of a cup of yogurt—he would say he spends maybe 5 minutes a day on this. Lunch he eats out—a tuna fish sandwich, Chicken Vindaloo, pork fried rice. This usually takes about 15 minutes. (That 15-minute estimate includes the time Ethan spends waiting in line to pick up his order.) Dinner is almost always something out of the microwave. Heat and eat: 10 minutes. Totaled, Ethan spends about 30 minutes a day getting himself fed—or 8 days and nights a year. This means that from now until the end he will be spending about 320 days at one sort of table or another. He should probably add another 50 days to that to cover the occasional long lunch or dinner with friends. And another 20 if he continues to know Stewart Dolnick, the slowest eater on the face of the earth. As he foresees both possible additions and subtractions, he will consider them a wash. (As he gets older fewer meals, longer to prepare, etc., etc.)

Walker is a fine writer, a gifted, committed, and sensitive stylist—but if any of us really envy him anything, it is, I think, his agent, Melissa Cox. It will be interesting to see what sort of space he gives her in this memoir. (It has always been Walker's practice to run early drafts of his stuff by her. I can't imagine ever doing such a thing.)

I have started corresponding regularly with a man named Aaron Kettle. He runs a library (The Richardson Library) in Lakeville—a small town out in western Washington. He is an interesting character. (I might look a little more closely at him if I ever get the hang of this nonfictioning stuff.) The library is devoted to a writer I have never heard of, a man by the name of Phillip Richardson. It reportedly houses all of Mr. Richardson's papers. (It also evidently holds a number of Mr. Kettle's manuscripts.)

John worked late the other night on one of his complex (and lucrative) litigations—the Kendall thing (CEO with a persecution complex suing a criminally malicious board for wrongful termination). John offered his attending parale-gal—Victoria Something—a ride home. Normally she takes the bus. Turns out she lives with a pair of variously invalided parents in a heartbreakingly cheesy apartment—one of those boxy, prefabricated, thin-walled, in-need-of-painting places. It started John thinking about his life. He forgets sometimes the enormity of his good fortune.

The Charter Gallery is almost a parody of what a gallery is expected to be these days—a clean, cold, white, minimalist clinic where you could hang a painting or perform an appendectomy. The only thing missing is the icy scent of industrial-strength disinfectant. Ms. Young was also pretty much what you would expect—efficient, formal, thin, dressed in black. She gave me some background on Charter himself, but as for finding him that fateful morning, she didn't really have anything to add to what was already in the file.

WINE

If you are experienced and not hurrying it probably takes about 30 seconds to open a corked bottle of wine. A bottle a day means Ethan is spending at least 3 hours a year on this simple task. It doesn't sound like much until he multiplies it out. In the time he has left—from now until the end—Ethan will have spent more than 5 full days and nights doing this. If he starts buying wine with screw tops, he could open a bottle in about 1/3 of the time. He would save 2 hours a year or—from now until the end—about 3.3 days, time he could invest in doing something generally considered ameliorative—like sit-ups.

Dog-Related Items

Ethan feeds his Boxer Toby twice a day. There is not much involved here—maybe 3 minutes a time, which works out to 1.5 days a year or 60 days total from now until the end. Taking Toby for a walk—well, that is something else. They go out for 15 minutes or so at least 3 times a day—that is 274 dog-walking hours a year. Add maybe an extra hour a week playing ball in the park for the next 40 years, and you get 543 days and nights of exercising Toby. (Of course sadly it will not just be Toby. It will be Toby and his replacement and his replacement's replacement.) Ethan spends at least 2 hours a year taking his dog to the vet (Now to End = about 3 days). Apparently one gains a few days of lifespan owning a pet—let's generously estimate 50.

At Work

Time wasted talking with David West—approximately 15 minutes a day, 5 days a week, 49 weeks a year for 30 years (assuming he will still be there when Ethan retires) equals from Now to End approximately 75 days. Approximately twice that amount of time is wasted every week arguing with Stephen Shield—or 150 days. Ethan spends probably an hour a day working and reworking figures he has already done, which adds up to about 306 days. He spends at least 10 after-work hours a year in nervous fretting over the semi-annual audit—or about 12 days. (He is excluding all but the last of these numbers from the current calculations as the hours and days in question have already been accounted for under the general topic of "Work.")

Kettle sent me a picture of The Richardson Library. It looks inside very much like a Victorian livingroom—fireplace, overstuffed chairs, drop-leaf tables, oriental rugs, oak bookcases. There are photographs on the walls taken by Mr. Kettle himself—almost all of them of people wearing hats. There is a large portrait over the fireplace, a silhouette, a slender man in a fedora. It is identified as a photograph of the late Mr. Richardson.

❧

I wonder what Justin thinks about when he looks up at the night sky. Is it all outer space and rocketships to him?

❧

As for your wayward fan, I agree a certain sort of friendly concern would be normal under normal circumstances, but as we both know, the circumstances as they pertain to Ms. Keen are not normal. Your worry about the rightness or wrongness of a strategic withdrawal seems pointlessly punishing.

❧

Walker made some amusingly judgmental comments about his self-destructive behavior the other day. Seemed amusingly oblivious to the fact that this behavior—the behavior he was disparaging—was, in fact, the reason he was asked to do the memoir. His work is one thing, but he wouldn't be camped out with his advance, his notebook, and his sheaf of questions were it not for his flamboyant disintegration.

Natalie is back from her weekly visit across the street. Isabel has, once again, rearranged the furniture in her livingroom—or more accurately (as she is too old to pick up an armchair let alone a couch) has hired someone to do it. It is a regular thing this cosmetic renovation of her life—what one does in widowed grandmotherhood.

I think good ole Dr. Hyde is at his best when he is complaining about the architecture of the novel and its pandering to the demands of plot and at his worst in provocateur mode when he is sanctioning plagiarism (as "creative appropriation") and trotting out that gussied-up truth-is-relative trope. I don't really know if he believes what he has been saying or if he just enjoys the attention seeming to believe it brings. A little of both I think.

It is different out here in the suburbs being suddenly awakened in the early a.m. by automatic lawn-sprinkling systems as opposed to downtown where it was drunks, car alarms, and garbage trucks.

❧

Kettle has sent me a thumbnail sketch of Phillip Richardson's life. Apparently Mr. Richardson was at one point committed to a mental institution where he received electroshock treatments. Divorced, broke, alcoholic, his books no longer of much interest to anyone, he killed himself at the age of 52. (He drove his car into a bridge abutment. Recovering what was left of him from the smoldering pile of mangled metal took the better part of an afternoon.) Kettle is working on a biography. He has been working on it for ten years.

❧

There is something peculiar about Natalie's larynx. It's constricted. You should watch her swallow a pill. She might as well be trying to swallow a soccer ball. It's quite a production—gulping, gagging, arm flapping. Me, always on alert, ready to try my first Heimlich.

❧

I was reading a story the other day—a famous story, one that is always mentioned when discussing the writer. It was predicated on the fatal illness of a friend, and it struck me how many notable stories in general are similarly predicated.

(I could think immediately of four. You who have read more broadly could recall many more I suspect.) It bothers me—writers feeding off others' misfortune. And yet here I am with David Charter.

⌖

I took the train down to Portland for a little three-day vacation. It is without question the most civilized way to travel—no interstate traffic, no airport angst. The two things I envy Europeans most—cafe culture and the railroads.

⌖

I think Walker is planning to interview me. He asked the other day for a brief bio. I sent him the following:

Stephen Styles: Only child. Born in Seattle. Father a lawyer. Mother a CPA. Likes cold and overcast. Wishes he played the piano. Is impatient and easily stressed. Does not like crowds. Neat not sloppy. Analytical, anxious, honest, pessimistic, easily tired, and stubborn. Relates effortlessly only to his wife and to his dog, a beagle named Bobby.

The problem with this nonfiction stuff for me centers in large part around the obligations I invariably feel toward a living subject. They are different—inhibiting, disruptive—from the obligations I feel toward fictional characters. There is a debate out there among those who still believe in debate about what is basically a betrayal of trust—an argument that claims "special" privileges for the writer. I can make these arguments to others when I am on the spot (a greater good, art for art's sake), but not in the end to myself. This puts me, I think, at a sort of perpetual disadvantage when it comes to this genre.

5

I confronted the scales this morning. I've put on a few pounds—but not really that many. Mostly it just seems to be a matter of where they are ending up. The distribution of things seems to be changing—and not for the better.

❧

According to my copy of the police file, newly-divorced David Charter (his wife left him for an abstract expressionist) had recently started dating. He employed a computer service. He had been out twice—once with a woman named Diane Kelby and once with a woman named Samantha Long. It was three weeks after this last date that he was killed. As an intrepid investigative journalist, I will be interviewing Ms. Kelby soon.

❧

John and Allison have new next-door neighbors—the Hamptons. They bought the Douglas house. Mr. Hampton (Ted) is a marketing guy for an athletic shoe company. Mrs. Hampton (Rebecca) runs a small interior-design business. They have a daughter Hailey's age who is, unfortunately, prettier than Hailey—though, of course, neither John nor Allison acknowledge this as they are still in the process of armor-plating Hailey's self-esteem. If for some reason they are compelled to refer to this girl's prettiness, they downgrade it with an adjective. A "plastic" sort of prettiness is John's official position. Allison refers to it as a "characterless" pretty.

❧

My expectations for this interview are not high. Not because of Ms. Kelby—I know nothing about her—but because of me. I can't imagine I will do a very good job of this even though I've studied the interviewing book. Natalie—she can get a life story just with the open way she says hello. I can't imagine what this is going to provide in the way of cogent and compelling copy.

Olivia, the vegetarian who cuts Natalie's hair, has started volunteering at an animal shelter. She dog-walks and foster-cares. She is pathologically committed to thinness and doing good, to being assessed by all as gentle and virtuous. She has put herself on an emotional diet of positive and selfless thought.

The route Natalie and I invariably take into town goes right through the middle of a cemetery. We are practiced and very good about not noticing—not noticing the hillside of head-stones. We black out from Barnes Ridge (a hideous condo-minium community) to Skyline Blvd—the turnoff to the interstate. If we are conscious of anything, it is the decora-tive firs.

I met Diane Kelby at a restaurant near her apartment. It was a place from another time—BC (Before Cholesterol). Large laminated menus. Everything comes with gravy. I have no idea how a computer could have matched her (wild eyes, fright-wig hairdo, talks with her hands) with Charter. I suspect simple fraud, but I am not ruling out the possibility of an unfortunate and grievously flawed algorithm. Ms. Kelby did not have that much to say about Charter, but she did have a lot to say about herself. She has, it seems, led a complicated and dramatic life—one that involves heavily both the legal and medical communities. There were imprisoned progenitors, connections to organized crime, rare genetic disorders. I don't think much of what she told me was true. I'm still trying to decide if this makes her interesting.

It is hard to guess how much time Walker will spend on the dissolution of his marriage—quite a bit, I expect, as neither party seems overly concerned about exposing the intimate details of their emotional and financial ups and downs.

Another fascinating note from Aaron Kettle. He says he was once Mr. Richardson's student, that he took a class from Richardson—who in the last few years of his life had taken to supplementing his dwindling book income with cash from writing workshops. According to Kettle, Richardson left a considerable amount of material behind. Kettle has been having a terrible time organizing a coherent account.

Spending time with my figurer of figures again.

TELEVISION

Ethan watches ½ hour of local and ½ hour of national news a night—a total of a little more than 15 days and nights over a year. At this rate, over the next 40 years he will spend 608 days and nights doing this. He expects he might miss a night or two here and there, so he is going to round that number down to 600. It is important to stay informed, but he could cut the fluffy human-interest stuff they put at the end of these broadcasts—say the last 5 minutes or so—stories like "Little girl reunited with lost puppy," "Woman watches Mardi Gras parade from the same spot for 15 years," "Man donates lottery winnings to pair of worthy charities." He would pick up 60 hours a year doing this—almost 100 days by age 75.

Ethan watches an hour-long dramatic series maybe 4 times a week. That is about 8 ½ days and nights over a year. That works out to approximately 346 days and nights by age 75. These drama series keep getting worse. It is a trend that Ethan expects to continue, so he imagines his total watching hours will probably decrease over time—to say maybe 250 days and nights.

He watches a ½- hour comedy series maybe twice a week—about 2 days and nights over a year. From now to the end—that would be about 86 days and nights. These series are already so bad that he doesn't think they can deteriorate any further, so he will leave this number unadjusted.

Three nights a week Ethan watches movies—usually about 2 hours each—about 13 days and nights over a year or 520 days and nights by 75. These movies are also getting worse, but as Ethan will be growing steadily less active and less likely to find something else to do, he expects this number will remain pretty much the same.

When it comes to watching sports, outside of the occasional tennis match he watches almost only football—mostly pro, not much college. He averages, he thinks, about 2 games a week at 3 hours each for 16 weeks. That works out to 4 days and nights over a year or 160 days and nights by age 75. That number could go up some as they continue to periodically lengthen the season.

It's the second time this week that Justin has been awakened by nightmares. It seems to be a collection of various monsters with razor teeth and blood-smeared snouts. Apparently decapitations are also involved. What do you think is going on? Is it his upbringing or his diet? What does he need: more love or less pepperoni?

I looked briefly at Mary Gardner. She writes mostly about either her cats or her mother. Not for me, I'm afraid. She is brilliant but emotionally retarded. Her paragraphs can be inspired, but the thing as a whole is invariably ruined by a glaze of anthropomorphic slop. Not poignant. Pathetic.

Today I interviewed a friend of Diane Kelby's for background. It seems Diane has a jealous, testosterone-addled ex-husband. This ex-husband's name: Andrew Voss.

Walker has unearthed an interesting communication with Melissa, his agent, in which he gives letter grades to a handful of his short stories—these are A's, these are B's, these are C's, and these are E's. Did you notice there are not any D's? An interesting aesthetic—a thing was a failure to Russell if it wasn't at least average. I haven't thought about it much, but I don't think I agree. I think a C is an E as well.

I spent the evening shopping for a new refrigerator. It wasn't as much fun as it sounds.

I know it is a difficult thing to imagine—neither of us really think of ourselves as having an effect on someone else (someone, that is, who is not our wife), but I agree there is something in these most recent communications with Ms. Keen that is worrying. She is obviously interested in something more than your opinion of a systematized metalanguage.

•❦•

Kettle thinks there are things missing from his Richardson archive. He suspects the mystifying and difficult Mrs. Richardson (the ex) is holding on to a few of the more important notebooks.

•❦•

Reading

Time spent reading stories in the newspaper or online that Ethan does not have a need to read—stories that are neither entertaining nor edifying: 30 minutes a day. That adds up to about 7 days a year or 280 for the full run. Stories like "Robber with knife scared off by woman with hedge shears," "Boy on class field trip jumps off Golden Gate Bridge," "Angry girlfriend sets vehicles on fire at car dealership."

What about books and magazines? How many novels does he start and not finish—at least 1 a month. Some he decides not to read fairly quickly, others he is a third of the way through before he knows it is not for him: average amount of time Ethan spends reading before he stops is about 3 hours. That is 1 ½ days per year or 60 days and nights of reading the wrong novel over the next 40 years.

Cleaning

Ethan spends about 1 ½ hours a week dusting, cleaning, and vacuuming—about 3 days and nights a year. He will spend a total of about a 120 days and nights doing this from now to the age of 75. His apartment is small and, although he is slightly germophobic, he thinks he could reduce this some—say 15 minutes a week, which would work out to ½ day a year or 20 days over the next 40 years. Unless, of course, he starts making more money, gets married, and gets a larger place—in which case this number could go up dramatically. (Ethan has certain standards.) He thinks he will leave this figure at 120.

Friends

Ethan would estimate that he spends about 8 hours a month visiting with friends he would rather see less of. He probably can't reduce this by much—not and still have them as friends. He probably spends another 8 hours a month with people he sees enough of and 8 more hours with people he would rather see more of. Total time spent with friends per month is about 24 hours. That works out to about 12 days and nights over a year or 480 days and nights by age 75.

It is an interesting dichotomy—most people think of Walker as "literary" because he doesn't offer happy endings while a few of us—you, me, a couple of others I could name—think of him as "not literary" because he doesn't offer unhappy ones.

Kettle is worried about how his work as biographer will be received. He wants his book to be both informative and artistically satisfying. He does not want to appear overly obligated to those who have offered him material. He wants to be judicious, but not so judicious as to be tiresome. He is worried his motives for everything (what he includes and does not include) will be questioned and questioned impolitely.

Do you know anyone who has gone deep-sea fishing—anyone who has *wanted* to go deep-sea fishing?

Big news. Hyde is moving to a new apartment. It's a pretty regular sort of thing with him—this restless search for the perfect place. Long-ago divorced, he travels light. Few (if any) of your standard re-locator's tormenting logistical concerns. I envy him that. Anyway...we will be hearing plenty I expect about the soon-to-be discovered shortcomings of this new sanctuary. Occasionally the issues for him are aesthetic, but mostly they are acoustic. (Hyde was once examined by an audiologist and told he had unique ear canals.) Thin walls. Minimal insulation. Don't get him started on the myriad insufficiencies of our local building codes. He says the place he is living in right now is about to fall down—that any time a neighbor slams a door, he has to straighten the pictures in his livingroom.

Walker is being very thorough about the book deals—about his advances and his royalties. Whatever else we ever say about him, we will always, I think, begrudge him the money.

For all the work he has done on the bio, Richardson remains a mystery to Kettle. He was apparently an extremely odd man in a number of ways—but also, in an equal number of ways, spectacularly ordinary. His qualities did not average out in any way that made sense. The sum of his parts did not make a feasible whole.

It is not the calendar that tells me it is summer, but the shock of that first bikini.

6

John has just grinned and chit-chatted his way through another office party. They are, according to him, invariably worse than regular parties. There are a number of reasons—the guest lists, the amount and quality of alcohol available, the fact that they are almost impossible to get out of. The ones around his place—birthdays, retirements—seem to be getting more and more elaborate. There are balloons, streamers, noise-makers. No one but a satirist really wants to see a lawyer in a funny hat.

❦

Samantha Long denied knowing David Charter when she was first interviewed by the police. She was ashamed of having used a computer dating service. Her friends would not have understood. I'm interviewing her on Wednesday.

❦

Allison is worried about Justin. She says he is getting harder-headed by the day. It's true. If he makes up his mind about something he just doesn't seem to be able—or should I say willing—to unmake it. This obstinacy does not bode well for the future. Allison thinks they will be completely estranged by the time he gets his driver's license.

❦

"Lotion"...the word itself is lotion—moist and soothing.

❦

Walker is covering familiar ground—the vicissitudes of the short-story writer compelled by critical, personal, and professional expectations to write a novel. He is telling the story of his long and unhappy struggle with *Face to Face*, the increasingly ugly arguments with Julia, the increasing use of alcohol.

Have you ever wanted to drive a bulldozer? I have not. But, of course, now as I think about it...well...

I have befriended—for the time being anyway—a nonfictionist in the hope of picking his arid empiricist's brain. His name is Mathew Metcalf. I know you have read a few of his things. I asked him for some tips the other day. He counsels immersion. Move in with your subject if you can—eat, sleep, and play with them. And if immersion is, for one reason or another, not an option? So far no answer.

Preliminary Overview of Ethan's Calculations

<u>Total Days Left Available: 14,600</u>

Debits and Credits:

-5 pulling corks out of wine bottles

-4,240 sleeping

+600 cutting out 1 hour of sleep a night

-400 unspecified damage to health due to lack of sleep

-2,573 working

+1,286 unspecified benefits of working

-744 commuting plus deleterious effects of stress

-52 brushing teeth and going to dentist

-106 showering and washing hair daily

+25 washing hair every other day

-50 shaving daily

+25 shaving every other day

-150 exercising

+37 unspecified benefits of exercising

-370 preparing and consuming meals

-20 continuing to have the occasional meal with Stewart Dolnick

-280 reading pointless news stories

-606 dog-related (feeding, walking, taking to vet)

+50 unquantifiable health advantages accrued by owning a dog

-12 worrying about semi-annual audit

-120 housecleaning

-60 reading the wrong novels

-600 watching television news

+60 avoiding human-interest stories on the news

-250 watching television dramas

-80 watching comedy series

-520 watching movies

-160 watching sports

-480 visiting with friends

Total number of days left to Ethan to make something reasonable of himself: 4,805

Time spent preparing these figures: 1 hour 45 minutes. Thinks he should do a more detailed analysis as time permits.

According to Kettle, Mrs. Richardson (the ex) has been making his job harder of late. As Phillip's literary executor, she has been slow to answer questions and grudging with referrals. She petitions constantly for previews of his work. "The more women you know in particular," he says, "the more confused you will be about them in general."

✦

Lunch with Jonathan Davis. It is only when I listen to stories told of bird-watching that I realize just how exciting golf can be.

✦

There are lots of things about Natalie that simply amaze me—her optimistic streak for one. That this should seem such a strange and notable thing to me is, I know, an indicator of my own predisposition.

✦

Instead of doing what I should have been doing this morning (working on Charter), I read *The Citrus Trees*—a long story of Carl Lightman's. I was struck again by what everyone is struck by—the frenetic outlandishness of his imagination, the strange worlds he creates. It is inspired stuff without question, but what is left after the marveling? It is miraculous monkey-business signifying what—that these days one must set their hair on fire to get anyone's attention. The work is in the end, I think, really just a form of cartooning. Lightman is gifted, he oozes originality, but he frustrates me.

Alan, we have over the years talked about many things, but I realized the other day that we have never really talked about breakfast food. So what is your position on pancakes? I cannot imagine you would be against them, that you would favor waffles or condone a buckwheat version.

When is the last time you went anywhere (outside of your house) barefoot? I used to always be barefoot. I never am anymore. For me, the last time was 6 years ago on a beach in Hawaii. It couldn't have felt stranger.

Allison is thinking about redoing their kitchen. She cannot decide—granite or tile. Her list of pros and cons have been no help at all.

❧

I met Samantha Long at Cascade Park. She was throwing a stick for her dog—a Labrador named Judy. We had a brief talk about her brief encounter with David Charter. She described him as a nice enough man, but not exactly her type. She found him rarified, insufficiently masculine. She mentioned giving Charter's name to Teresa Knight, a distant friend—a distant friend who is interested in art. This name is not in the file that Kevin Cain gave me.

❧

Someone related in some way to Isabel has a vegetable garden—which means, of course, that Isabel has been given approximately 5 times as many zucchinis as she can use. This means, of course, that when Natalie returns from her weekly visit she has 4 times as many as we can use.

❧

Always wondered which sort of parents were most destructive—those who were not meant for each other, who fought and were miserable, or those who were meant for each other and didn't have the time or the inclination to divide their affections.

I read a line of Walker's the other day describing his inebri-
ated self as "a curious compound of hostility and amiability,
of gloom and glory." Seems to me a pretty good description
of the un-inebriated Walker as well.

Additional items that Ethan should consider for numerical
analysis:
    time spent listing to music
    time spent filling out forms
    time spent waiting for various repairmen
    time spent sick in bed
    time spent worrying about a Republican takeover of the
Senate.

One of the things Kettle says he admires about Richardson's
work is its bluntness—its willingness to be cranky, annoyed,
and critical. "He felt no obligation to present himself as
Richardson of Sunnybrook Farm."

⌀

Miserable morning. Textual system malfunction. I am grappling again with grave disappointment—with intimations of mission mortality.

⌀

I ran into Laurie O'Dell the other day. She is one of the people who thinks it is charming to be superstitious. She thinks it makes her unusual and interesting. It's a form of accessorizing.

⌀

I wish you luck in exiting the epistolary relationship with Ms. Keen. We have all heard stories about the difficulty of such a maneuver. I'm afraid your skill as a wordsmith is of no importance. There is nothing you can say that she will not take the wrong way if she wishes.

Why is it always considered a good thing to have a positive attitude. There are times—many of them—when having such an attitude is nothing more than an expression of delusional mentation.

Walker has finished with his separation from Julia and is moving now into those first few years of "teaching"—those innocent years when he applied himself.

I had a cup of coffee yesterday with Brian Snow. He has always been for me a sociological phenomenon, a cultural measure—the averagest of average men. Everyone else seems to some degree a deviation. Married to his high-school sweetheart, he has two children (a boy and a girl), a steady job, and everyone he knows owns a Ford.

I have decided to scrap the Ethan Davis project. I have never been able to shake my worries about it—my suspicion that its destiny was to devolve into a meaningless mire of capricious computation.

Mrs. Richardson (Linda), needing a small cash infusion, let some of Phillip Richardson's letters be published a couple of years ago, but they were heavily edited by her—a fact that did not go over well with either the academics or the general reading public. Kettle says he has always wanted to like her, but that it has become a harder and harder thing to do as he is confronted again and again with suspiciousness and intransigence.

I talked with Hyde this evening. His news is of palace intrigue. Dr. Eaton, Chairman of the English Department (and long-time ally of Hyde's in the daily to-and-fro of departmental politics), is leaving for a more lucrative (if somewhat less prestigious) post. His likely replacement is rumored to be the dreadful Dr. Milburn, a pretentious, theory-addled pedant who Hyde expects will make life in the well-waxed halls of academe as unpleasant for him as possible. Tenured, his job is safe—what is in jeopardy is the nurturing collegial ambience.

Do you own an actual tool box? I do. I bought one when we moved here. It sits mostly unopened in the garage, but I am very fond of it. It makes me feel ready for anything. I have in the past 10 years used only a hammer, a screwdriver or two, and a pair of pliers. Everything else—well, it is as good as new. Even the items I have used—the hammer, the screwdrivers, the pliers—look like new because they have not been used often, and when they were used, it was not for anything significant or heavy-duty.

Sometimes I know an idea is not going to work right away. Other times it may take me months to come to that conclusion. Sometimes I will recognize it suddenly—in response to a phrase, a conjecture, a stray character. Other times it will involve a complex and gradual sorting out of fundamentals. Sometimes I will persist because I do not want what I suspect to be true to be true. I am careful about allocating limited resources of energy and attention. To waste either is upsetting. I always work with trepidation, with the suspicion that I am ignoring some problem that I should not be ignoring. I invariably find myself trying to fix something that can't be fixed.

⁘

This freakish snowstorm has been a misery. How long do you think before some young up-and-coming literatus desperate for material uses it as the backdrop for an autobiographical short story about a disintegrating marriage?

⁘

Metcalf is packing for a road trip. (He is doing a piece about a rag-tag band and the clan of fanatic misbegottens who follow them.) He has a tacky tent, a ratty sleeping-bag, a cooler full of beer. Says it will be the first time he has slept on the ground since high school. We commiserate—that we are no longer the hairy-chested frontiersmen we once were.

It is easier, I think, to find a rich man who is humble than to find a beautiful woman who is kind. Natalie is the exception that proves the rule.

7

Hailey and Justin think their parents have formed some special alliance against them. Whatever problems John and Allison might have with each other, they come together against these innocents—come together to thwart their dreams and desires, to make their lives more difficult than those of their friends.

⚘

I've been looking into this Teresa Knight—the woman who Samantha Long gave David Charter's name to. She is forty-four, divorced, and the mother of one (a daughter, Mia, who has just gone off to college). She is a heavy drinker with an extreme sensitivity to the issues of aging—things that a gym membership, psychological counseling, and high-dose anti-depressants have not been able to address. She has had several surgical procedures. (One was successful, two were not—jaw-line, mouth.) She has a history of mental problems and institutionalizations. Having lived the past four years with a teenager probably didn't help.

⟡

Olivia, the woman who cuts Natalie's hair, is seeing a psychic. She has been seeing one (or another) for years now—a psychic from whom she takes advice. What interests me about this is Natalie's reaction. She hasn't had one. She has known about this for some time, about the psychic, and yet she continues quite happily to let this woman manage her do. If Bill, the one-legged guy who cuts my hair, had told me something like this I would have been out finding a new barber the next day. How could you trust such a person's judgment about anything—including about how much to take off the top.

⟡

Allison has been catching me up on the latest. She likes to share admonitory fables—motivational stories of husbands behaving badly. She and Amy have a friend named Kara. Apparently Kara's husband has been having an affair with a woman at work. (He is an optician.) Both Amy and Allison have had a hard time believing it. It's just not the sort of thing this man would do as he is by nature a rectilinear sort of person, a moralist. What has apparently made it even more difficult to believe is the woman involved—she is not young, pretty, seductive, or blonde.

I have started making notes for another novel—this one about a magician. I am calling him Aidan Powell.

AP, it seems, has grown tired of amazing people. He has had an attack of conscience—some sort of epiphanic conversion. He has developed a new relationship to the idea of illusion. A stage magician who has focused mostly on close magic (sleight-of-hand work—coin and card tricks), he has changed his act. He has started to explain away the magic of his magic. He performs a trick and then shows the audience how it was done. Reactions to this new act have been mixed, but mostly they are negative and hostile. Does he continue or does he stop? He continues. Why? Because he is worried about the fate of fact in the world today. The problem, of course, is that this new act is not popular. It is losing him money—a lot of it.

Ah, neighbors—they get you thinking. For instance, lately I have been trying to decide which is the more inherently intolerable—the five-year-old or the nine-year-old? I think a case can be made for either.

As much as Mrs. Richardson suspects everyone else's motives, everyone else suspects hers. There have been legal moves to get the literary conservatorship reassigned—something Kettle has not yet but might in the near future support.

The older you get the worse you look, but the better you eat. It amazes me now to think how little attention I paid in my twenties to breakfast, lunch, and dinner.

I had a very interesting chat this morning with Teresa Knight. She said yes, she had gone out with David Charter a few times, but that things just hadn't worked out. She said she had found him nice enough and that had ironically proved to be the problem. Nice enough would have been nice enough all other things being equal, but all other things were not equal (she was going through a bad time) and nice enough was not nice enough—it was cruelly mocking. It forced her to acknowledge to herself that she wanted more. Charter had inadvertently forced her to face the prospect of an arid and unhappy future.

Note from Metcalf. He is on the road headed for a Midwestern fairground and a byline in a big-time glossy. He says the focus of his piece will probably be more on the followers than the followed.

Do you know anyone who owns a parrot? I do not. They are incomprehensible to me—parrot-owners—disturbing, a species of person I do not understand.

Walker has hit on an inspired explanation for the rapacious self-indulgence of those first few post-divorce years. It was the consequence, he says, of "nervous desperation." How does one reply to that? Yes, Russell, we understand. All is forgiven. He is trying, I think, to preemptively mitigate the damage that could be done to his reputation by the as-yet unwritten memoirs of a half-dozen stray liaisons.

Tim Price, the man who lives behind us, manages the claims department of a small insurance company—a company that has (with some overly-rosy actuarial estimates) gotten itself into trouble and begun laying people off. Everyone is tense. No one knows who is destined for dismissal. Tim is especially worried. (He has mortgage problems and a second child on the way.) The target of entrenched and powerful adversaries, he feels particularly vulnerable. He has in the past been willing to make allowances for the individual idiosyncrasies of certain people working under him (Daniel Brett, for example—a collector of lizards), but now he is looking at these oddities a little more closely. Adjustments to a new, efficient, totalitarian order are being quietly suggested. Daniel, who displays a particularly virulent form of recalcitrance, is a special problem. He has been tolerated mostly because he is good with charts, and for some reason he is a favorite of the much-feared Bethany West in accounting. Tim would like to ship him off to another department (to another supervisor), but he doesn't feel he can.

❦

Magician notes.

Aidan sees himself leading a movement in magic—one that eschews the manufacture of illusion for the manufacture of explanation, one that replaces a democratic unknown with, among other things, an undemocratic lesson in neurobiology. Aidan's new act is a sort of reverse-engineered version of Magic Realism—it is Real Magicalism, the boiling down of extraordinary or inexplicable events into a philosophically good-for-you gruel of quotidian verifiables. He feels there has been an almost adolescent flight from rationalism, from logic and facts, toward the fictitious, prestidigitational power of wishes, whims, and beliefs.

❦

Hyde moved into his new place yesterday—which means another housewarming party. I think this is, in part, one of the reasons he moves so frequently—so he will have an excuse to produce one of these things. I have been invited, but I don't want to go. Try as I may, I am just not a party guy. I don't really know how to talk to people. I spend too much time talking to myself, to the page, to whatever it is I am trying to do. It is ineptifying. I have only so much energy. Most of it goes into daily living, into maintaining emotional equilibrium. What is left goes into literary projects, into getting this or that paragraph right.

I've been to at least three of these do-das. They are always the same. Someone who for some reason is trying to impress either an individual member of the ensemble or the ensemble as a whole will show up with something expensive and French (which I will do my best to get more than one glass of). Someone else (actually several someone elses) will show up with flowers. Vases will be improvised. It's always a demoralizing adventure being sealed into a small room with fifteen intoxicated academics. The air is thick with muted malice, filled with polysyllabic witticisms and the smell of damp tweed.

⋅◉⋅

Tim had a meeting this afternoon with Patrick Masters and a pride of mid-level bean-counters. The "committee" (Patrick is the company's heartless, granite-jawed, no-nonsense enforcer) would like him to work up an appraisal of several projects. Tim suspects they are after a scapegoat—something they have done has gone wrong, and they are looking for someone to saddle with the blame. He was told that "concerns" had been expressed about his recent job performance. These "concerns," of course, were not specified.

Aidan is suspicious of his own motives. He continues to champion demystification because he thinks it is the right thing to do, but he worries about a hidden, less romantically noble agenda. He seeks out a psychologist to discuss the matter.

Metcalf has finally arrived at pastoral venue. The festival, he says, runs for three days and resembles on first impression all others of the genre—crowded, chaotic, cacophonous. He has set up his tent on the periphery of what looks like a Somali refugee camp and has located the tribe he is interested in—the disciples of that rag-tag group of no-names. He has been recording conversations that may not be all that scintillating, but when transcribed, he says, they will go a long way toward fulfilling his contractual obligations—vis-a-vis word count. In his forties he has been accepted as an exotic. Shared a couple of blunts with his zealots. Wrote an ode to peanut butter.

⚬❦⚬

Finally after X number of years (I don't think Walker has decided yet on how many to claim), *Face to Face* was finished and sent off to his publisher.

⚬❦⚬

Yes, like you, I have a bad feeling about Ms. Keen. I am afraid your story is going to get complicated.

⚬❦⚬

Before our joints gave out Natalie and I played tennis and racquetball together regularly. Now we play backgammon and do the crossword. When it comes to the crossword I'm lucky. Natalie is brilliant and can spell the paint off a pool cue. We race through the *Times*—me slipstreaming all the way. Backgammon is another story. N is an optimist. She has a romantic's resistance to the idea of "odds." At present she owes me something in the neighborhood of three million dollars.

Chris Young, my painter friend, wants me to go with him when he visits his wife tomorrow. They are separated. She (Whitney) moved out a year ago. Chris has been unhappy ever since. All his paintings are of dark and empty spaces. He is still attached. He has hopes there might be a reconciliation. He thinks there is a chance, but he wants a second opinion, an outsider's unemotional assessment of the situation as it exists today. This is not the sort of thing I am comfortable doing, but it seems I have agreed.

I talked with Mia Knight about her mother. They are ostensibly estranged. They have complex and incompatible ways of engaging with the world. Mia has had things pierced. She finds her mother menacing and manipulative.

I have been looking through the psych lit for studies of people who want to be magicians—people who want to amaze strangers with what they know are elaborate lies (aka novelists). So far no luck.

I don't really think I know anyone any longer who is involved in a significant way with water—no swimmers, no boaters, no skiers—no one who finds themselves regularly in oceans, lakes, rivers, ponds, or pools. I was in all of those continually as a kid. As an adult—not so much. These days if it weren't for a shower, I don't think I would ever get wet.

I heard Justin was complaining to his father the other day about never having had a broken bone. He said it was embarrassing at his age to never have had anything in a cast. It suggested a certain sissy-ishness.

Back to work on Charter—or should I say on my arbitrary assemblage of devices.

It is heartening to see Walker's book—his best—fail (as I have seen so many fail myself), knowing as we do that in the end it will have its day, be discovered, read, and honored extravagantly. It is a fate I like to imagine from time to time for maybe half of my own orphaned production. (It was interesting to see how many titles the book had before it got the one we know. I can't imagine negotiating such a detail.) Anyway...now the wretched scrivener moves on—on to the famous who blurbed and befriended him.

8

Natalie's birthday. Late. Full of wine. Reading a piece in the *New Yorker* about the vicissitudes of the trade. The writer (McPhee, I think) said fiction was harder than fact because the fiction writer moves forward by "trial and error" (possible book title) while the fact writer works with a certain body of "collected material" (another possible title). At the moment I don't seem to be moving forward in either genre.

I talked with a woman by the name of Janet Casali. She was once housed at Alder Creek with Teresa Knight. She remembered Teresa as "intense." She told me Teresa had been at another institution (Shady Brook), but, accused of tampering with a patient's food, she was transferred. There is no paper trail to be excavated as the people at Shady Brook did not feel they could prove the accusations conclusively.

Allison is getting more and more worried about Leah. She seems to be getting more and more depressed. Allison says it is upsetting as there seems to be something inexorable about it. She says it is harder and harder to go to lunch with her, but she is afraid to stop. Leah is no longer having one glass of wine, but three or four—which makes lunch way too long, her friend becoming simultaneously philosophical and incoherent.

Who prefers silver to gold? Parrot people perhaps.

Metcalf has been back for a while now and is working up his notes. He seems especially eager to do an impromptu séance justice. Also, he has a handful of life stories to polish.

He is planning, he says, to take a couple of detours on his way to the closing ceremonies—one to the festival's first-aid station (overdoses, a broken arm, the birth of a baby—a girl spontaneously named Trudy) and one to his formative years, to a drum-set bedizened bedroom with its walls and ceiling painted black.

Back with my magician.

Aidan, who teaches magic to supplement his income, has had an affair with one of his students. (Liked the unconditional adoration.) Samantha, his wife, has found out. (How?) She wants to move on, to forgive and forget, but she can't quite seem to. The affair has been over for a while now (two months), but it continues to take up mental space.

Allison has decided to refresh her Italian. She bought a recording and a phrase book.

Walker has been focused lately on one of the more insufferable subjects of belle letters—the disreputable goings on at our favorite writers' colony.

Hailey is on a new mission. She thinks her family should be eating better—that, for instance, they don't get enough fish oil in their diets. (It is supposed to do wonders for their brains—she is nothing if not subtle—and their triglycerides.) One of her friends, Alexa, is the daughter of a proselytizing nutritionist. John and Allison will be listening to a lot of this sort of talk for a while.

Mr. Kettle is a recreational wood-worker. According to his wife, he often smells of cedar.

John is becoming, he thinks, a more and more careful person. He would like to find something wrong with that, but he can't—not really. The admonitions he imagines sound self-congratulatory, preening, and romantic.

Tim has started looking for someone in his department to hand blame off to after Patrick Masters hands it off to him. It is like a relay race. Who doesn't he like? There is Phillip Greenwood—but Phillip's life is a miserably hard one right now (medical issues, in-law issues, crisis of faith, low blood sugar). Tim would feel terrible if he got him fired. What about Liam Tickner? Tim doesn't feel one way or the other about Liam. He has little concern for what happens to him.

Count the flashing lights in David Blake's oeuvre—police cars and ambulances. You will be amazed.

I went with Chris to his almost-ex-wife's apartment this afternoon. Officially we were there on an errand. Chris was picking up a carved wooden box. He wanted to paint a picture of it. Whitney had agreed to loan it to him. (It belonged to her grandmother. Whitney took it with her when she moved out.) We had coffee and a pleasant little chat before we left. Nothing revelatory, I'm afraid.

Have you ever thought seriously about buying a monkey? I have. Of course, I never will. When it comes to avoiding the work I am supposed to be doing (work on Charter, for instance), I have no shortage of excuses. If I owned a monkey how could I ever do anything but attend to it.

Scene:

Cold February morning. Samantha, the magician's wife, is getting breakfast ready for the children. The boy, Thomas (thirteen or fourteen), is a slouching sad-sack of hormones and complaints. He is sullen and wears a perpetual expression of disdain. His slightly younger sister, Sophie, is hostile—unhappy with her latest haircut and the grade Mr. Epps gave her in English. Neither of these children like each other nor do they like their parents. Neither of these parents like each other nor do they like their children. Alliances are formed and broken hourly. Samantha is especially dispirited. She feels like Sisyphus—rolling his rock up the hill just to watch it roll back down again—getting the children off to school just to watch them return with their bad attitudes and their accusations of inadequacy. Samantha tries to hide her feelings about these children (she suspects it would just make them more unpleasant), but she does not do a very good job of it.

Additional information about Samantha:
She has always wanted to learn how to ice skate.

•◦•

I read a few more of Walker's pages today. We have arrived, finally, at his first breakdown. Desperate and exhausted after his heroic struggle to finish *Face to Face*, he disintegrates into manic irrationality. It is the breakdown he uses to great advantage in *Mental Weather*.

I have always had a feeling that Walker would have liked to have had at least two more hospitalizations. They are like award citations. They decorate a certain sort of CV.

The essential problem for me is that I am a hedonist. It is much more fun to plan a novel than to actually write one. In the planning it is all pyrotechnics and promise—no grinding, eviscerating disappointment.

Apparently it is our turn to get new neighbors. I am a little worried because of the proximity. Mr. Hound-Dog face is gone, which is good, but I don't know yet who will be replacing him. I would like to say the chances are 50/50 that it will be an improvement, but somehow that doesn't seem to be true. Actually it seems more like the chances are 20/80 that it will be an improvement. New neighbors are like peach pie—almost always a disappointment. Natalie hopes they will be nice, that we can have them watch the house when we are out of town. My list of wishes are always the same: 1. that they don't have children, 2. that they don't have a dog, 3. that they don't play musical instruments, 4. that they are not social.

Scene:

Aidan is in his classroom holding forth on the "center deal," one of the most difficult and treasured moves in card-sharpery. It is all about touch, he says—about developing touch, a sense that is in most cases woefully underdeveloped. He demonstrates an exercise program, a sort of gymnastics for your hands that isolate and strengthen the finger muscles. There are all sorts of strange flourishes involved. It is difficult (especially at full speed) to differentiate one gesture from another.

Brian Murphy dropped by to see Tim this morning. He had heard about Tim's meeting with Masters and was worried because it affects his department if Tim is in trouble. He asked Tim to talk with Mark Wilkinson, another middle-manager—a veteran of many such engagements. According to Tim, bright-eyed Brian is a little too much of a morning person.

Vis a vis Ms. Keen, my answers are "yes" and "no." Yes, you were too friendly. No, you did not move quickly enough to extricate yourself. I think you are more interested than I am in having people like you. You must have discussed this with Dr. Cartwright.

I ran into Della Lowe at the communal mailboxes this afternoon. Della is a widowed friend of Isabel. She lives four houses down from us. I avoid her as much as I can. She is one of those gardenia-scented ladies who will talk to you endlessly about the weather and the cute things her cousin has done.

Now it is page after page about the star treatment that Walker and *Face to Face* received—the catered meetings with advertising, the high-profile interviews, the prestigious magazines teasing previews.

I started out this morning trying to be productive, but ended up being myself—unproductive, frittering, despondent. Am stuck again trying to mask my contempt for the contempt of intellectualism—which unmasked seems to be invariably misunderstood as an uninflected endorsement of an imperial elitism.

It has been one of those days. I have been thinking about my life—what has been more important: the things that have happened to me or the things that have not. The father I had or the mother I didn't. How important was it to not be tall? As important as to not be small? To not have been born a woman or an Asian, to have good posture and symmetrical features, to be middle class, to work in an office and not on a farm? What if I had stayed at home instead of running away? What if I had joined a union? What if I had studied computer programming instead of English Literature, had one sister instead of no brothers, had a taste for beer but not for wine? What if I were a Catholic and not an Atheist, belonged to a club or two instead of none? What if I was a Republican and not a Democrat, a golfer and not a photographer? What if I was ambitious instead of not, patient instead of not, easygoing instead of not, extroverted instead of introverted, an optimist instead of a pessimist, afraid of want but not of heights, could speak French or play a musical instrument? What if I was stupid or smart instead of average, comfortable instead of uncomfortable?

I am thinking about writing an essay for Terry Boxall at *Balderdash*. He was kind enough to ask for something a while back. It would be a different sort of thing—an essay about an essay I would almost certainly fail to write in response to my initial impulse; an essay that would have been, had I been about to write it, well worth a certain sort of reader's time—an essay not about foreign travel, substance abuse, psychological abuse, or life-treating illness, but about the chronic failure that is part of this business.

People in general are inclined to put a lot of faith in their intuitive judgments; writers are usually even more so inclined. It is not simply because this is an easy way to reason, but because these sorts of judgments have a mythic quality—they are considered, rightly or wrongly, essential and authentic. I think if I were to describe my trajectory as a writer, it would be from someone who placed a lot of faith in his intuitive judgments to someone who honors them but is wary.

My guess is things probably would have gone better for Walker if he hadn't pretty much insisted that all of his new friends be alcoholics.

9

We got a call from Natalie's mother last night. Apparently her father had some sort of episode on the golf course yesterday afternoon. He was taken to the hospital. This is not the first time, but it seems it was a significant "heart event." (Doctor-speak designed to frighten and reassure simultaneously.) They are keeping him overnight for observation and, of course, another half-dozen expensive tests. Apparently there is some sort of surgery that will eventually be required.

⌖

I turned the information I had about Teresa Knight over to the police this morning. As I understand it, they are bringing her in for questioning. I have no idea if Ms. Knight was involved—I can only say that it is not unimaginable. It is going to be quite a while, I think, before we find out how this ends—before I find out how this book ends. I don't really mind. I have a lot of work to do on the thing.

For some reason John is excited about Justin's new friend, Thomas. Thomas, it seems, has a microscope. He does scientific experiments in his room—experiments with beakers, test-tubes, and litmus paper.

It is a perennial question for some, but not for me. *Face to Face* is a very good book, but I do not believe that producing it has exempted our illustrious author from the standard practices of civil behavior. It has not given him a grant of social immunity—the right to be a horse's ass.

Fortune tellers are one thing—it's the people who believe in them that are something else. Those are the people who frighten me, who fill me with despair. They will outlive us all—outlive you, me, and everyone we know—and sometime in the next five billion years before the earth is incinerated by the sun, one of them will be elected President of the United States.

❧

Tim introduced me to one of the "characters" in his department—a part-time order-verifier named Sarah Graysmark. Spectacularly unattractive. Many chins. Perfectly crazy. Looks like Oscar Wilde just before he died. Favors stretch pants and acrylic cardigans. Logorrheic. Is always having some sort of disgusting physical problem—something is always draining or getting infected.

❧

I am tossing the magician idea. It seems to me too archly issue-laden and allegorical. The subtextural discussion of conventional fiction seems fated to deteriorate, to become instead a subtextual (or not-so-subtextual) discussion of conventional religious belief. Also, there are—inevitably— the card and coin tricks. It would be, I suspect, a very tedious thing trying to make them interesting on the page.

Funny how flavors stay with you—warm Dr. Pepper, for instance. Belgian chocolate.

Natalie asked me this morning why I was frowning. I said I wasn't, that this was just the way my face looked now. She said she read somewhere that it was good for one's thinking to frown, that it made you more analytical.

Did you ever read Walker's third novel, *Strange Comforts*? I think he has a thunderstorm on every other page.

Coffee with Metcalf. I don't really know how helpful he is going to be in the long run as he seems committed almost exclusively to a participatory form of journalism. Tips on this approach are of little use to me. He is off next week to cover a Body Art Exposition in Pomona. He is unmarked at the moment, but I suspect he will not stay so.

Tim heard a rumor today that he was going to be sent on a consulting mission to St. Louis. He will have to accept the assignment as it will, in all likelihood, be presented to him as a reward.

Funny talk with Hyde. It got me thinking back about those fervid undergraduate days when intellectual interests could, occasionally, rival erotic ones. I remember the discovery of one book in particular, a heretical tome by Dr. Mathew Floyd, a polyglot professor from New York, critiquing the social sciences, attacking the presiding mechanistic interpretation of we lowly humanoids as empirically passé, bashing brilliantly the great boogeyman of my baccalaureate: behaviorism. I can remember viscerally how excited I was to have a complex, Heisenberg-haunted argument against determinism, a defense for the treasured proposition that I did not *have* to be me.

⁂

I don't know about these interviews. I think to be good at this sort of thing one needs to feel entitled. I, unfortunately, do not.

⁂

The first thing I have to do if I am going to write an essay for Boxall about an essay I will almost certainly fail to write is to ignore all of the essays I have not written before. There are quite a few as I seem to sit down regularly with the intention of doing this sort of a thing. The basic idea is that writing an essay will be fun and good for me and not take very long (especially compared to writing a novel or doing this Charter thing). I know from the past that none of these things is ever true—it won't be fun, good for me, or done quickly—so the first thing I have to do if I want to do this piece is to find a way to ignore this. It is not as difficult as you might think.

⁂

It looks like we have reached the bread-and-butter chapter of Walker's memoir where he treats us to a catalog of his sexual conquests—a registry of pointless assignations festooned with a lot of backhanded boasting about his new-

found desirability. It's this one after this one after this one—
until at last we stumble upon Mrs. Walker #2.

⚬

I miss Ethan and his abacus.

⚬

Out in the backyard with Bobby. I toss a tennis ball for
him. I marvel at the uncomplicated pleasure this affords
both of us.

⚬

I met the new neighbor. He owns a boat dealership. He
admires money and outdoorsiness.

⚬

Right now Ms. Keen claims merely to be annoyed. Before
long she will be openly hostile. I know it will be difficult for
you. I hope you are ready for it. You might have Dr. Cartwright up the dosage on a prescription or two.

I can feel it coming on. I am nearing that place where I invariably lose interest. The only way to write a book is quickly, and I don't seem to be able to do that any more—not quickly enough anyway.

It is quite obvious that Walker thinks his whole life would have been different (better) if the National Book Award hadn't been a near-miss.

When is the last time you found a dollar bill laying on the ground? I think I was in my teens. The world these days is vacuumed by needy homeless.

Natalie is back from the salon. That means a half-hour of hair talk—also, of course, the latest on her stylist's efforts to master the pan flute.

I don't know if I ever told you anything about John's grandmother—she committed suicide. She left a note—nothing much, nothing accusatory or hateful, just a terse expression of existential hopelessness. It was preserved and passed down to his mother, who just recently passed it on to his sister. I asked him what she was going to do with it. He said she didn't know. She was thinking about simply throwing it away.

Here is a list of my most recently abandoned essays:
Anglophile or Francophile
My Life as a Scientist
The Gym
Revenge
Third-Person Narration
On Preoccupation with Physics
Portrait Painting.
I bow my head in reverent silence before the unfathomable mystery of the fizzled inspiration.

❧

Has anyone in Walker's generation ever passed up the opportunity to complain about Updike?

❧

Have you looked in your wastepaper basket lately? What do you think is the ratio of things you have thrown away to things you have not. The number I would bet is surprising, but I am not sure it is one that a struggling writer really ought to know. As the thickest trauma counselor will tell you, there are things that once seen can't be unseen.

❧

I think I have an idea for another novel.

❧

The two things I most vividly remember learning how to do are type and drive a stick-shift. (In distant third is learning how to dance—sort of.) I remember virtually nothing at all about diagramming sentences. Natalie, of course, can tell you everything you need to know (and more) about gerunds, predicates, and participial phrases.

•••

I have eaten at McDonald's only once in my life—a confession that separates me from how many? I still do not, at this point, have any interest in ever eating at one again. It has been, I think, a couple of decades since I have had a hamburger of any kind. It would be easier to explain this if I were a vegetarian, but I am not.

•••

I think I know what is coming next in the Walker book— professional exculpation and a paean to psychotropics.

•••

I had my picture taken today for an updated bio. It's something Aaron, my diffident publisher, has been pretending to need. The photographer, nice enough, was a proselytizer—an aesthete who eschewed studio lighting for ambient, which means, I suspect, that in the end I will not look anywhere near as brooding or mysterious as I should have liked. At one point he suggested I rest my chin in my hand—you know, the classic *Thinker* pose. I do not believe he was intending a parody. I declined—politely.

I, like you, have little interest in dreams—mine or anyone else's. That said, last night's was memorable—everyone in it wore a surgical mask.